Me and Arch
and the Pest

Me and Arch and the Pest

John Durham

illustrated by Ingrid Fetz

FOUR WINDS PRESS • NEW YORK

Published by Four Winds Press
A Division of Scholastic Magazines, Inc., New York, N.Y.
Text Copyright © 1970 John Durham
Illustrations Copyright © 1970 Ingrid Fetz
All Rights Reserved
Printed in the United States of America
Library of Congress Catalogue Card Number: 73-105338

For Scott

ONE

Some folks say our dog's name is Ritter von Bulow the Third. And I guess that is his fancy name. That they put in the book, and all.

But Archie and me, we know his real name. It's Pest. We named him right and nobody else can tell us. Don't we feed him? Don't we walk him? Don't we brush him out and even cut his toenails? Didn't we save him from them dognappers? You bet we did. Who else got a right to call what his name is? Especially some funny German name nobody understands.

I'll tell you how we got him, old Pest. And all the other things that happened. Archie and me was out this Saturday. Arch, he came by my house and yelled for me that mornin'.

Now me, I lived in this teensy little old house down in South L.A. That's almost in Watts, but not quite. It's a nice little old house. That got vines all over it, with these wild-looking purplish flowers. Only trouble is, South Los Angeles, it's mostly colored. Or my momma, she thinks it's trouble. She been moanin' about livin' in with the colored ever since we moved out from Georgia, three years ago.

But me, I like it. Heck, *Arch* is black. And me and Arch are just like *that*. Well, he's not black, actually. Actually, he's this nice smooth coffee color. Coffee with lots of cream. Only reason I mention it, is how my momma feels.

That mornin', I was back in the kitchen, having a little cornmeal mush and tea, like. When I heard old Arch first. Out front on the sidewalk.

"Bit!" old Archie called. I could hear him. From out on the sidewalk. "Hey, Bit! Come on out!"

"Who's that yellin'?" my momma, she called from the livin' room. "What's that awful noise out there?"

"I'm comin'," I yelled to Archie.

"You hear me, Bit?" my momma said. "Who is that? And stop that terrible screamin' in this house. You hear me?"

Momma, she's all right. She gets these sick headaches and this gastric distress, but she's nice, most of the time. It's just that she don't like the colored. You know. Hell, she grew up in Georgia. What you gonna do with a lady grew up in Georgia? Can't tell her nothin'. She won't even listen. So that morning I just sailed past her and out the screen door.

"You, there, Bit, you whoa!" she yelled.

But I was gone. Five minutes and she'd forget about it. I knew that.

"Hey, man!" Arch said, when I came out the door. "Whatcha doin', all that time? Huh?" He hit me on the shoulder. Kind of hard.

"Look out, man," I said. "You'll kill me with them powerful blows." I hit him back. Harder.

"You musta got stronger overnight," he said. "You couldn't hit like that yesterday."

"What's goin' on, dude?" I said.

He held up this old beat-up bat. "Let's hit a few," he said. "Over at Ella Wheeler Wilcox School."

"We can't do that, man," I said.

"Why's that?"

"With them powerful muscles of yours," I said, "you'll knock out picture windows a block away."

"We got to take the chance," he said. "The Dodgers need me."

"Oh," I said. "Yeah. I forgot about that. What's a few picture windows?"

We dogtrotted all the way, just to loosen up. We throw my ball back and forth as we go.

"Hey, man," I say, "how are things with us?"

"We all right, old buddy," Arch, he said. "Like that."
He held up two fingers.

"How much bonus we gonna get?"

"A hundred thou apiece," he said. "Besides the two
cars."

"What kinda cars they gonna be?"

"I thought a Lincoln Continental for starters. You
know, for pickin' up the laundry. And maybe a Rolls-
Royce for when I wants to put on the dog."

"I don't know," I said. "Maybe a Lincoln. But them
Rolls. They just plain ugly to me."

"Your taste, it's all in your mouth," old Arch, he
said. "Folks that know, they got Rollses."

"Folks that know," I said. We was joggin' along,
like I say, and it come out like, 'Fo-holks tha-hat know.'
"Them folks bother me."

"Like what you mean?"

"Well," I said. "Like teachers, see?"

"Yeah," Arch said. "What about teachers?"

"Well," I said. "Teachers are supposed to know
things. Right?"

"Right."

"But look at English teachers. They always tellin'
you how to talk right. Right?"

"Man, they are."

"Like, you got to not say got. Right?"

"Right."

"But *folks,*" I said. "They all say got. Like my poppa. Now, he says, 'I got no money.' But the English teacher, *she* say he can't say got. See what I mean?"

"Man, I know it. Way she says to talk, it don't feel natural. Your poppa, he a natural man."

"Right," I said. "He is *that.* So, how am I suppose to talk?"

"Me," Arch said, "I talk the way folks expect. You know?"

"What you mean?"

"Well, in English class, I talk the way the lady wants. But out here, where people is, I talk the way folks talk."

"I try to," I said. "I mean, I try to do that. But it mixes me up a little. Then, there's you black people."

"Yeah," Arch says. "There's us." He grins.

"Now you talk a little bitty bit different from my poppa. So me, I'm all mixed up, 'tween you and the teacher and my poppa."

"Thing to do," Arch said, "is to just open your mouth, baby, and let it roll out."

"Maybe," I said. "But then Old Lady Garrity, she wrinkles up her nose." Old Lady Garrity, she's my English teacher. "She makes faces when I just let it roll out."

"You want to be a natural man," Arch said, "you got to expect a little nose-wrinklin'."

"That is for dadgone sure," I said. The thing is, I want to be a natural man, all right. But I don't want folks like Old Lady Garrity makin' faces at me. I want her to smile when I talk. Because Old Lady Garrity, she's downright good-lookin'.

We got out on the grass playground at Ella Wheeler Wilcox. Arch, he's up first. He gets up there and I get way out. Because, man, he hits 'em. He whanged one out to me, way up there. Way up there against the smoggy blue. It was sailin' down to me, nice and easy. When something happened. I was reachin' up for it, you know, just like pickin' a raisin out of a fruitcake. When, Zip! Zap! Pow! Bang! Here comes this black and white streak. It sailed past my left shoulder and up and grabbed the ball.

"Watch out, man!" old Arch, he called. But too late. That big old dog *had* that ball. He caught it seven feet up. Neat and easy, he caught it. And he went loopin' on down that field. It took me a while to see him, he was goin' so fast. He run down past Arch and circled him. He come back and circled *me*. Just zippin'. He cut two figure eights like that. Then he stopped, just halfway between us. The ball was still in his mouth.

He looked at Arch, first. Then he looked at me. Then he dropped the ball on the grass. He put one big old paw on it. And he just looked at it.

Let me tell you about that dog. First off, he was big. I mean. You *think* big. But he was *big*. He was one of them police dogs, you know. A German shepherd, some calls 'em. His face, it was black, with little silvery white marks around the eyes. His tail and his legs, they was black, too. But all the rest of him was this kind of silvery white. You know? Like he been dusted with snow. He was a beauty, I tell you. But *big*.

"Look who got the ball," Arch said.

"You look."

"Who gonna get it?"

"You. If anybody does. Because I ain't."

"You chicken?" Arch said.

"You know it, man. I can cackle and I can crow. I might even lay you a egg or two."

"You think he's mean?" Arch said.

"Me, I'm not even gonna consider it," I said. "He's there and he's got my ball. He wants it that bad, he can have it."

"Ah, man, I just hit *one*."

"Hit away," I said. "I'm just the fielder."

"I think I gonna wait a while," Arch said. "He might get tired of standin' there."

"He don't look tired to me. Does he to you?"

"Not very." Arch, he sat down, holdin' the bat handy.

That big old dog, he looked at me. He looked at Arch. Then he barked.

"Sounds kind of playful," Arch said. "Don't it?"

"Maybe," I said. "You go play with him."

The dog, he picked up the ball in his mouth, then. He trotted toward me. Why pick on me? I thought. The dog come to within ten feet of me before he dropped the ball. He dropped it, then he looked up at me. He barked once. He barked twice.

"He wants to play," Arch said.

"Well, I don't," I said. "Leastways not with no monster like that."

The dog picked up the ball again. He come to within five feet of me and look like he was just comin' on *over* me. Then he dropped the ball again. And he looked up at me and *grinned.* Yeah. Just like a man. Like any human. And he barked twice.

"Oh, well," I said. "All right." Truth is, I was kind of tired of bein' chicken. He wasn't nothin' but a dog. I told myself that. So I went over and picked up the ball. Right out from under his nose. And I hauled back

15

and threw it up to Arch.

That dog, I tell you. He got down there almost as fast as the ball. I never seen nothin' move no faster. He slid up to Arch like an old pro. Then he set there and watched while Arch threw the ball up and hauled back the bat to swing.

Arch connected, way he always does. And that dog was gone. He lit out. He was down there, settin', waitin' when that ball started down. I didn't even try to outfield him. Hell, I know when I'm beat. No human being ever caught a ball no neater, either. He caught it. And he brought it over to me and dropped it. Then he looked up at me and grinned.

"Smart alec," I said.

He barked, twice.

"Oh, all right," I said.

I picked up the ball and threw it down to Arch. This time I had more guts, when Arch hit a high one. I tried to beat out the dog. And I did. Course, he took the ball away from me. Soon as my feet hit the ground, he had it out my hand. And he trotted up to Arch and laid it in his hand. Then he waited, nice and polite, till Arch hit it down the field.

That went on for a hour. Till I was all tuckered out. I was draggin'.

"Hey, Arch," I yelled. "You field 'em for a while."

"No, man," he said.

"Well, then, let's quit." I looked at the dog. He was settin' there. Waitin' for Arch to hit another one. *He* wasn't tired, not one little bit. "You sure can break up a game," I said to him. "You're a pest, you know that?"

"Let's go down to the Taco Lita," Arch said. "I got some money."

"Okay," I said. We started off down the street. The dog, he just set there. Lookin' after us, like a man, his big old eyes bright. He just watched us.

"By-bye, pest," I said.

"He's a *dog,*" Arch said, "that dog is." He looked back. "Look at 'im. He's a *dog.*"

"He's a pest," I said. "You wasn't out there with him."

"He could take a man apart," Arch said.

"That's another thing tired me out," I said. "Just wonderin' if he was goin' to. You know?"

We didn't see him again. Not till the tacos was ready and I had mine raised up for the first bite. Then there he was. Settin' there in front of me. Grinnin'. And lookin' hungry.

"Aw, come on," I said to him. "Pester Arch this time."

18

"Here, dog," Arch said. "I ain't a stinge. I give you one of my tacos." And he threw him one.

"Looks like we got us a dog," Arch said.

"You," I said. "You got *you* a dog. Cost twenty dollars a month just to feed one like that."

"I wouldn't mind," Arch said. "I never had no dog."

" 'Sides," I said. "He got to belong to somebody."

"You think so?"

"Sure. A dog like that. *Some*body owns him."

"Well, if we just walk off," Arch said. "And he follows us. Now, that ain't stealin', is it?"

"I don't know," I said. "I guess not. Naw. That ain't stealin'."

By this time that first taco was gone. It was gone quick, in fact. In fact, it took two bites. And he was standin' there, Pest was. Just lookin' hungry. And grinnin'.

"If I buy three more tacos," Arch said. "And I just walk down the street, you think he'll follow me?"

"Looks likely."

"And that won't be stealin'?"

"I don't think so. Not a bit. You can't help what *he* does. Can you?"

"Naw, man. How can I help it?" Old Arch he went up to the window. "Give me three tacos," he said.

And that's the way we got Pest. I'll tell you in a minute the trouble we had keepin' him. And after that, I'll tell you how he saved old Arch's life. And mine, too.

TWO

"Not no dog, never," my momma yelled. "Nossir. Nossiree, boy! You ain't keepin' *no* dog."

"You seen that dog," I said. "You seen him out there, tied up. Ain't you?"

"I seen him," Momma said. She turned and looked at me, narrow. Then she looked at Poppa. He was settin' on a kitchen chair, takin' it all in. "What you gettin' at, boy?" she said.

"You looked at that dog out there," I said, "and you got scared. Now didn't you?"

Momma put her hand at her throat. "Why, I don't know," she said. "No. Nossir, I ain't scared of *no* dog. That ain't why."

"It ain't nothin' to be ashamed of," I said. "Now, take me. I first saw that dog, I was *scared.* Puredee frightened. I tell you. I was."

Poppa kinda laughed. My poppa, he's taller'n a tree and twice as smart as my momma. He knowed what was comin'. Poor old Momma didn't. How come is it that men is smarter than women? I always wondered about that.

"Yes ma'am," I said. "I was scared. It's only natural, take a dog that big. You know it? Anybody'd be scared. Now, wouldn't they?" I said all this to Momma. She knew somethin' was comin', but *what* she didn't know. "Now just admit you was a little scared," I said. "Just a teensy bit."

"Well," she said, "maybe just a smidgin."

"All right," I said. "You was scared. Wouldn't other folks be?"

"Why, I guess so. That dog would scare anybody just a little."

"And most folks it would scare a *lot*. Right?"

"I don't know," she said. "I guess, maybe."

"Say he was barkin'," I said. "And comin' at you with them big white teeth. Anybody, he'd be scared. Wouldn't he?"

Momma was seein' it, that big dog comin' at her. "Lord God," she said, "I guess they would."

"Now, Momma," I said.

"Yeah?"

"You know you always sayin' this."

"Sayin' what?"

"That you wish Poppa didn't work nights. Don't you?"

"I said that once, maybe. Maybe twice."

"Okay," I said. "Now wouldn't you feel just a little bit better with Pest around?"

"Who?"

"Pest. That's the name we give him, Arch and me. *He'd* make you feel safe."

Momma shook her head. "Naw," she said. "No, he wouldn't."

"How come, Momma?"

"He might come after *me.* That's how come."

"You give him his food, say. He wouldn't come after you. He's a smart dog."

"Maybe," Momma said.

"Then," I said, lifting a finger. "Then there ain't no good reason I can't keep him. Is there?"

"Oh, yes there is," Momma said.

"How come?" I said.

"Because you just ain't goin' to have no dog, never. That's how come."

"That was good, Bit," Poppa said. "You did all that just fine. You argued your case as good as a lawyer."

"Yeah?" I said.

"Only one trouble."

"Yeah?"

"You lost it."

"I guess," I said. "Women," I said.

"Yeah," Poppa said. "Momma," he said.

"I ain't your momma," Momma said to him. "I'm *his* momma, but not yours."

"That's right," Poppa said patiently. "Now listen," he said.

"No," Momma said. "No dogs. Not never."

"Listen to me."

"No."

"If he feeds the dog," Poppa said. "And takes care of it."

"No," Momma said.

"And has a chain to keep it on. You don't use that backyard."

"No," Momma said.

"Why?"

"Because," Momma said, "I'm scared of that big old thing."

"You just said you wasn't. Didn't you?"

"I said I was, a smidgin."

"That's not enough," Poppa said. "Not to keep the boy from havin' his dog. That's a good-lookin' dog out there."

"Who gonna buy the feed? He'll eat half a cow a day, that thing out there."

"Bit?" Poppa said.

"Yessir."

"Bit, you get yourself some little ol' job. Carryin' boxes out of a grocery store. I don't care what."

"I'll try," I said.

"You pay for his feed," Poppa said. "And you can keep him."

"You wait, James Lee," Momma said to Poppa. That's Poppa's name, James Lee Merriwether. "You wait. I gonna get even with you. You'll see."

"Aw, now, Momma," Poppa said.

"I ain't your momma," Momma said. "And I'm gonna get even with you. You'll see. Just you wait."

THREE

"How come you don't get a job?" Arch said to me.

"Same reason you don't."

"Man, I am totally wiped out," Arch said. He set down on the curb in a loading zone. "I bet we walk three million and five miles."

"The thing is this town didn't plan things right," I said. Me, I slumped down at the curb, too. "They got all them grocery stores too far apart."

"You mean all them stores what tells us they don't need no boys to work for them," Arch said.

"Those are the stores I have reference to," I said.

We was out on the street in front of the Majestic Pool and Domino Parlor. Old Pest, he was just sittin' there, too. Lollin' out this big old pink tongue, a yard long. We had him on this choke collar and leash. That I borrowed the money from Poppa to buy.

"He looks tired, too," Arch said. "Don't he?"

"He walked as far as we did," I said.

That was when this guy come out of the pool parlor. He was a kind of old guy, maybe forty. A heavy kind of man, with his stomach hangin' over his belt. And big arms and shoulders. A heavy head and big pale eyes and little tiny ears. He come out not lookin' at us.

But ol' Pest made him pay attention. He lifted his nose and sniffed. He turned and looked at the guy. He growled, real deep and low in his chest. And he lunged at this fellow. I almost lost the leash.

"Pest!" I yelled. "Hey, Pest! What's the matter with you?" I fell down and was slidin' on the seat of my pants. "Arch!" I yelled. "Help."

Ol' Arch, he grabbed at that leash, too. And together we managed to quiet down that dog.

This guy, this big, fat slob of a guy. He didn't turn a hair. He just looked around at me and Arch and Pest. And he kept on pickin' his teeth with this match. Then he got in this red Buick convertible parked at the curb. And he drove off. All this time Pest was lungin' and snappin' after him.

"Now why do you suppose he did that?" I said to Arch.

"I don't know," Arch said. "That guy was maybe mean to him once. You think?"

"Maybe," I said. I looked after that red Buick con-

vertible. "I know one thing, though," I said.

"Yeah," Arch said. "I know, too."

"We still ain't got a job," I said. "And my Poppa gave me to Tuesday."

"We still got one day," Arch said. "You think we gonna make it?"

"I don't know about you," I said. "But I am. Here, Pest," I said. "Come here, boy." Pest come over and licked my face.

"Hey," Arch said. "He's my dog, too."

"Did I say he wasn't?"

"You didn't *say* it," Arch said.

"I didn't mean it, either," I said. "Here, Pest," I said. "Give him a kiss, too." And sure enough, Pest did. He was a good dog, I tell you. Old Arch and me, we looked at each other. We was both thinkin' what a good dog he was. And both thinkin' that tomorrow, we'd have to take him down to the animal shelter and leave him. For good.

FOUR

Next day it wasn't no different. I bet Arch and Pest and me walked twenty miles. I bet we went into a hundred stores and filling stations and places. I guess it was three-thirty, four o'clock we sank down to a curb over on Figueroa.

"Man, we had it," Arch said.

"Looks like."

"You think your old man, he really gonna make you—"

"My old man says something," I said, "and he means it. He's fair but firm. You know what I mean?"

"I know," Arch said. "Yeah, I know."

Old Pest, he was watchin' us. He was watchin' us just like a man. Like he could understand. He come over and kissed Arch. Then he gave me a lick on the ear. Like he knew we was tryin' to keep him.

What do you think slid up in front of us, 'bout then? This big black and white slab of metal. And this fancy shield that says, "To serve and protect" on it. The red light went to turnin' and flashin'. And this cop leaned out the car window. "Hey," he says, "you boys got a license for that dog?"

Arch and me, we jumped just about three feet. "Man, yeah," Arch says, quick. "But we done left it at home."

The cop laughed. "You better just run get it," he says. "And make it quick."

Arch and me got a good look at him then. You know how cops, they all look alike at first? Then you give 'em a good look and they're some different, this one and that one? We got a good look at this guy and it was old Jimmy Hines.

"Hey, Jimmy," Arch says. "How's things?"

"What you boys up to?" Jimmy says. He grins. "Kinda scared you, huh?"

"Yeah," Arch says, and, "Yeah," I says.

Old Jimmy's just like a little kid. I mean, he likes flashin' that light and all that. He likes to sit behind that siren. You know? So Arch and me, we go along. "Yeah," we say.

"I hear you boys lookin' for a job."

Arch looked at him. "Who told you that?"

"Things gets around," Jimmy says. He's white, but he's a good old boy. His partner, he's a black, I never did know his name. He's all right, too, Arch says. "We hear you got to support a dog."

"That's right," Arch says.

"He is a beauty," old Jimmy says. "I never saw a prettier dog." Old Jimmy, he's from Tennessee, but he's all right, too. "I like to have that dog," Jimmy says.

"Looks like you can, if you wants," Arch says. "Because we ain't never gonna find a job. Looks like. Today's the last day."

"Yeah," Jimmy says. He looked thoughtful. "You guys try over at Zimmerman's pet store?"

"Pet store?" I say. "Where's that?"

"Over on Imperial."

"I told 'em you guys were sixteen," Jim says. "You are, aren't you?" He meant about the law in California that says you can't work till you're sixteen. Some law. "You are, aren't you?" Jimmy says. "Sixteen?"

"Today was our birthday," Arch says.

"Happy birthday," Jim says. "If I'da known, I'da brought a cake. And candles."

"They really want some boys?" Arch says.

"Sure. Two boys to clean up and feed the animals. And water 'em, and like that. You know."

"Hey, great," I say.

"You better get on over there," Jim says.

"You know it, man," Arch tells him. And we're off.

The way we got friends with old Jimmy, it was like this. Arch and me was hittin' balls this Monday afternoon, out in the street in front of Arch's place. And old Arch he really lays one out there. A long, low straight one. That hit a Ford headlight like it was aimed.

Now, most guys, they break somethin', they light out. And Arch and me *talked* about runnin', but we didn't. Arch said it wasn't right. So we stayed. We knowed the police would come. But we stayed. And sure enough, here come old Jim and his partner. Arch and Jim and this guy who owns the Ford, they talked it over. And Arch said he'd pay for the headlight, fifty cents a week. And he did. Ever since, old Jim, he sees us, we have a little talk. Like pass the time of day and that. You know.

Anyway, we got to Zimmerman's. And there was this lady behind the counter. She was real old, fifty or more.

"Hey, man, she looks mean," I whispered to Arch.

"Hush, man," Arch whispered back. "Who cares? We got to have the job. Ain't we?"

"We have got to have it."

We told Mrs. Zimmerman that Jimmy Hines sent us over. She looked us over through these big glasses of hers. Her eyes was black and hard as rocks.

"You boys don't steal," she said. "Do you steal?" She had this German accent. "You don't take things that don't belong to you?"

Arch and me, we shook our heads. "No ma'am," I said.

She gave us another long look. "And you work hard?"

"Yes ma'am," Arch, he said.

"You work two hours in the mornings," Mrs. Zimmerman said. "Six to eight. Cleaning cages. Feeding the animals. Giving water." She looked us over. "And two hours at night."

We nodded. I looked around. They was monkeys, six or eight of them. There was this thing I found out later. She called it a kinkajou. They was cats. And turtles. And mice. And rats. And parrots and other birds. And out back they was at least fifteen dogs, all kinds.

"You think you can do all this?" Mrs. Zimmerman said.

I looked around that place. And I thought uh-uh, I couldn't. But I looked at old Pest, and I thought un-huh, I could. "Yes ma'am," Arch said.

"Yes ma'am," I said.

"My August did it all," Mrs. Zimmerman said. "But now he is dead. He died two weeks ago. And by myself I can't do it."

"Yes ma'am," I said.

"So I give you five dollars a week."

Arch and me, we didn't say anything.

"Together," Mrs. Zimmerman said. "Five dollars together."

Arch and me, we looked at each other. It ain't much, not for all that work. But what's a guy gonna do? "All right," Arch said. And I nod.

"Then shake on it," Mrs. Zimmerman said. And she shook hands with both of us. "Tomorrow morning," she said. "At six sharp."

I groaned inside. Me, I like to sleep late. Arch gets up real early. But I like to sleep as late as I can. Lord God. Six o'clock in the morning. I looked at Pest and I thought to myself, you better be worth it, old dog.

FIVE

I told you I'd tell you how Pest saved our lives. And now I'll start tellin' about it. It'll take a while.

We been workin' at Zimmerman's for, oh, three, four weeks, I guess. We knowed all the animals by that time. We knowed the turtles and the rats and the mice. We knowed all the cats and the birds. And specially we knowed the dogs out back, in the cages.

They was a collie named Old Boy. And a beagle named Posy. And a Scotty named McTavish. And lots of other dogs. Me and Arch, we got to know 'em all. Like they was our own dogs. Me, I'm a nut about dogs. I wish I owned all the dogs in the world. I mean it.

Anyway, this one night, we finished inside. And we went out to the back, to feed the dogs and water 'em. I was givin' Old Boy, the collie, his meat.

"Hey," Arch says, "who's that over there?"

It made me jump. It was total dark out there. "Who's that over where?"

"In that car."

I peered out through the chain link fence. First, I couldn't see anything. Then I saw this here car. A Buick, I thought. With a guy in it, just sittin'.

"He's just sittin'," I says. "He ain't doin' nothin'."

"That's what worries me," Arch says. "Why's he just sittin'? On a dark street? He was *doin'* somethin', I'd know *what* he was doin'."

"He's maybe casin' the place," I says.

"What's he want?" Arch snorted. "A bunch of dogs Old Lady Zimmerman, she can't even sell?"

"It's true," I says. "She ain't doin' well here. I think she's worried."

"She ought to be," Arch said. "This place don't hardly do any business. You know?"

"Yeah," I says. "I thought she was just tight. But she's like the rest of us. She's puredee poor. That's what."

Out there in the car, this guy, he lights up a cigarette. He lights a match and for just a second I can see his face.

"Hey," I says, "that's the guy old Pest, he growled at."

"What guy?"

"In front the pool hall. You remember?"

"Hey," Arch says. "He was a mean one. Wasn't he?"

"Listen," I says. "You go on feedin' the dogs. Okay?"

"Sure. But why?"

"Me, I'm goin' back into the shop. Then out the front door and around the block."

"What for? You need exercise?"

"Arch," I says, serious, "I'm sneakin' up on that guy. To get his license number."

Arch laughed. "You know what? You're some kind of nut. You know that? Why you want his license number?"

"Because," I says. Because I just wasn't sure. It was kind of odd for him to be out there like that. At night. Just doin nothin'. "It won't *hurt* to get it, will it? Tell me what it'll hurt."

"Go on, then," Arch says. "Run around the block."

So I did. I went around three sides of the block fast. Then, the last side, I could see his car up there, in the dark. I snuck along, from tree to tree. There's somethin' creepy about watchin' another guy. When he don't know it, I mean. Specially at night.

I snuck up to the next to the last sycamore tree. Fifteen feet behind his car. Then I got down on my hands and knees. And I snuck up to the last tree. I stuck my head around the tree. You think I could see that license

number? I couldn't. I tell you, it was dark. Some jerk, he knocked out the only street light.

Well, I thought, you got this far. You can't stop now. So I got down even farther. I slithered out from behind that tree like a snake. I mean. On my belly. And I got right up to that back license plate.

You know what happened then. Don't you? The door, it opened. Lord God. Somethin' inside me jumped up a full mile. Me, I stayed there on the ground. Just breathin' fast. This guy, he gets out and stands up. He hawks and spits. He starts to the back of the car. I almost died. Right there.

But he turned around. He got back in the car. And he started talkin'.

"Robbie?" he says. "That you? Yeah. Yeah. I'm comin' on in." Then he started the engine and turned on the lights and moved out. He done it so quick that I could just get the letters and the first number off the plate. RBA3—that was all I could get.

"So what you get?" Arch says, when I got back.

"Most of the license number. I got to quick write it down. RBA3. That's what I got."

"The guy didn't do nothin'."

"I know that."

"Then why you want his license number?"

"He was talkin'."

"Man, everybody *talk*. Practically."

"But it was on a car phone. Or a radio. He says, 'Robbie? That you? I'm comin' in.'"

"That guy, he's a truck dispatcher. Or a cab man. Or somethin'. Lots of folks got car phones or radio."

"I tell you, Arch," I says. And I was serious. "There's somethin' down in me says to watch out for that guy. And I'm writin' down his number."

"Come on," Arch says. "Let's finish up and go on home."

SIX

Next mornin', Arch was there at the shop, waitin' for me. "I done checked," he says. "There's nothin' missin'."

"All right," I says. "But you checked, didn't you?"

"Yeah," he says. "It was kind of odd, all right."

"We got another problem," I says. "My old lady, she's givin' me a hard time about Pest." I had Pest with me, on a leash.

"What kind of hard time?"

"She don't want him around. She's got this little apricot tree, see? That she planted herself?"

"Yeah?"

"And Old Pest, he dug it up."

"Dug it up?"

"Yeah. Dug up the roots and killed the tree."

"Oh, shepherds are diggers," Arch says. "I read that in a book. That Old Lady Zimmerman, she had on the counter. This book."

"Well," I says. "He's got to go somewhere else, till she cools down. That's all. I couldn't even talk to her."

Mrs. Zimmerman come along then, to open up for us. "Hello, boys."

"Good morning, Mrs. Zimmerman." We say it together.

"Not so good. I couldn't sleep."

"That's too bad," I says.

"Worry, worry, worry," she says. "All night. About the shop. I don't know how long I can go on."

"You mean you might have to close down?" I looked at Arch. He shook his head, worried. Where would we get the money to feed Pest? Besides, she was a nice old lady. She really was. She'd pass by and pat us on the head, when we was feedin' the turtles, or somethin'. And she'd tell us stories about Germany.

"They anything we can do to help?" Arch says.

"Everything in the world I know about dogs," Mrs. Zimmerman says. "Everything. I should have a kennel someplace. But there's no money."

"I'll get to thinkin' about it," Arch says.

"He's a good thinker," I said. "And I'll try, too."

"Thank you, boys," Mrs. Zimmerman says. She laughed.

"Mrs. Zimmerman," I says. "You know that empty

cage out back?"

"Yes, I know it."

"Could we maybe keep Pest out there? For just a while?"

"Pest," she says. "What a name for a beautiful dog! Oh, I don't know."

"We'll feed him ourselves," I says. "Separate."

"I guess so," she says. "But another dog comes in to board, out he goes."

Arch and me went out back with Pest. "That's one problem solved," I says.

"For awhile," Arch says. "Man," he says, to Pest, "what gonna become of you? If we lose our shop?"

SEVEN

"How come you're fidgetin' so?" Momma pointed her finger at me. "Because it's eleven o'clock. Which is way too late for you."

"No'm," I says. "It's not that." I was walkin' the floor. "I don't know what it is. But it's not that."

"Is his forehead hot?" Poppa says to Momma. "He might be sick."

"How can I tell?" Momma says. "With him pacin' like that. It's enough to drive a person wild. I mean."

I cracked the knuckles on my right hand. Then on my left.

"Lordy, what a noise," Momma says. "Sound like he throwin' a bucket full of rocks into a washin' machine."

"There's somethin' wrong. Over at the pet shop." I grabbed up my plaid jacket. "I got to get over there."

From outside the house there come this terrible yell. My hair stood up on the back of my neck. "Hey, Bit! Bit!"

"Well, spit fire and save matches!" Momma says. "What in the big old blue-eyed world is *that?*"

"It's Arch," I says. "Somethin' has gone wrong. I knew it."

"You come back here, Little Bit," Momma says. "You can't go out into the middle of the night without even—"

But I was gone. Out through the door and gone.

Arch was standing out there on the sidewalk. Or not standin'. Kinda jumpin', from one foot to the other. "Bit," he says, "come on, man, hurry up!"

"It's Pest," I says. "What happened to him?"

"How'd you know?" he says.

"I don't know how I knowed," I says. "But I did."

"Old Lady Zimmerman called me up on the phone," he says. "Pest's gone."

"Gone where?"

"She don't know. All the dogs is gone. Every last one of 'em." He sounded like he might just cry. "Come on," he says, kind of tough, to cover it up. "We got to get over there."

The pet shop was all lit up. And inside was Mrs. Zimmerman and Jimmy Hines, the cop. And Jimmy's partner. Mrs. Zimmerman was cryin'. "Boys," she says. "We've lost all our dogs. Your dog and the dogs I was boarding. It's all *kaput*," she says. "Finished."

"Now, it's not that bad, Mrs. Zimmerman," Jimmy Hines says.

"And why not?" Mrs. Zimmerman says, wavin' her hands. "Those dogs are worth oodles of money. Oodles. And I have no insurance at all."

Jimmy turns and looks at us. "You boys didn't have anything to do with this," he says. "Did you?"

I looked at Arch, kind of scared. I hadn't even thought of such a thing. That him and me, we might be suspects. "Honest, Jimmy," I says. "I been home all evenin'. My folks was there."

"Me, too," Arch says. "Honest."

"What would anybody want with fourteen dogs?" I says.

"I can tell you that," Jimmy says. "There's been a lot of dognapping around lately. A lot of it. They take the dogs and sell 'em for laboratory work. Or pets. Whatever brings more."

"The dirty rats," Arch says. "Old Pest is too good a dog to get cut up in some laboratory." He *was* cryin' now. I never seen Arch cry before. Not even when he broke his finger on a throwed ball that time. He was *cryin'*.

And I was about to. I tell you. "Hey, Jimmy," I

says. "Are these big-time guys that steal dogs? With radios and like that?"

Jimmy looked at me careful. "I don't know," he says. "Why do you ask a question like that?"

I told him about the fellow was out there the night before last, in the Buick. I told him how maybe he was the one who Pest got mad at, that time in front of the pool hall. I told him that and I told him about the license number. "But that's no good," I says. "Because I only got the letters and the first number."

Old Jimmy, he looks kind of excited. "You didn't throw it away, I hope."

"Naw," I says. "I got it here some—" I started lookin' through my pockets. I got this wild feelin' when I couldn't find it in the first pants pocket. "Not there," I says, to myself. Then I dug into my hip pocket, where I keep my billfold. I took out the billfold and went into this secret compartment. While my back was turned to them all. And there it was. "Here," I says to Jimmy. "But what you gonna do with it?"

"They got this computer up in Sacramento," he said. "That can tell you almost anything about who owns a car. Even if you only got part of the number. We'll see."

Jimmy turned to Mrs. Zimmerman. "We'll turn this

over to our detectives," he says. "And we'll let you know, soon as somethin' comes up."

"Those poor people who own the dogs," Mrs. Zimmerman said. "What will I tell them?"

"Don't worry, Mrs. Zimmerman," Arch says. "We'll find those guys. We'll find Old Pest. And we'll find them other dogs, too."

"Thank you, Arch," Mrs. Zimmerman says. "You're a good boy. But I don't think there's much you can do."

"Old Arch is pretty smart," I says. "And I'm not too dumb myself. We'll find 'em."

Then Arch and me, we went out to look at Old Pest's cage. Just to make sure. You know? How when somethin' gone that you love? You go to make sure? Well, that's what we did. We stood there and looked at Pest's cage. And neither one of us could say a darn thing. We'da been sure to cry.

EIGHT

It was the next day, I guess. Arch and me, we was mopin' along Imperial. It was like somebody died. Like when my Uncle Will, he passed away from a cottonmouth bite. Or the jug he drunk to cure the bite. I don't know for sure which.

Old Arch, he'd try to talk about how the Dodgers was goin' to do next year. How the Giants, they didn't have a chance. But he couldn't keep it up. His eyes, they would get far-off. And his voice would kind of drop off. And he'd stop.

We even tried havin' tacos. Which is our favorite food, almost. Except soul food, and like that. But we couldn't eat. We was just kind of mopin' along Imperial, there. When up slud old Jimmy Hines in his fuzz wagon.

Jim and his partner just sat there lookin' at the two of us for a bit. "They appear kinda down in the mouth, don't they?" Jim says to his partner.

The partner, this black guy, he nodded. "They bottomed out."

"I guess you haven't seen that big ol' dog," Jim says.

"Nope," Arch says. "Them guys done stole him."

"Hey," I says to Jim. "How about that car?"

Jim's eyes kinda narrowed and wandered off. "What car?"

I looked at Arch. "He knows somethin'," I says.

"Now you looky here," Jim says. "Who said I—"

"You don't have to say," I says. "That look on your face. *It* says."

His partner laughed.

"You hush up," Jim says to him. "Just hush up."

"You never should have pulled up here," the partner says. "I wish I could get you into another poker game."

"You done won my fishin' rod money," Jim says. "Whatta you want? The kids' Christmas savings?"

Arch went over and leaned on the car. "Where is the guy?"

Jim made his face go hard-guy cop. "Can't tell you a thing," he says. "Not a blessed thing."

"Jim," I says, "you got to."

"If I knew anything," Jim says, "and I'm not sayin' I do. If I knew anything, now, it would be classified, like. Our guys would look into it. Them detectives."

"Would?" I says. "You mean they haven't done a thing yet?"

"I didn't say they had nothin' to not do," Jim says.

"Say that again?" his partner says.

Jim, he turned red. "Y'all know what I mean. What I mean is," he stopped. "I mean, they don't have anything to do that they ain't doing. Or I anyway didn't say we even know anything."

"You kids get that straight?" Jim's partner says. "Save up some money," he says to Jim. "We'll hold the poker game at my house. I'll buy the beer."

"You can afford to," Jim says.

"Well," I says, "how *come* they haven't done nothin'?"

"In L. A.," Jim says, "fourteen dogs is not no big thing. Not with banks bein' knocked over. And murders. And one or two other little ol' things."

"You know where that car is at," I says.

"If you wrote that address down," Arch says. He stopped.

Jim looked at him. He looked hard.

Arch looked off up at the sky. Which was smoggy. "And say you, uh, lost it," he says.

A little glint come in Jim's eye. "And?"

"Well," Arch says, "somebody might find it who'd

go out there and stake out the joint."

"You lookin' to get yourself killed?" Jim says. "Why, those guys are hardened, professional criminals. They're downright *mean*."

"How do you know?" the partner says.

Jim didn't even look at him. "Hush," he says. And then he says to Arch, "You'd just go over there and look? And come back and tell me?"

"Sure," Arch says. And when Jim looked at me, I nodded.

"Now, I don't want you boys hurt. Even in Beverly Hills—"

"How about if I loan you some money?" the partner says. "To invest in some poker?" He looked at Jim plumb disgusted.

"Oh, just hush completely up." Jim was red as a beet.

"We're goin' over to the pet store," I says. "Now, if you just lost that little ol' slip of paper over there. Say out back. Around the dog pens."

"You wouldn't," Jim's partner says.

"Who says I wouldn't?" Jim gave him a hard look. "These boys here, they care about that dog." Jim stopped for a second. "Me," he said, "when I was a lad, I had a dog like that. That I felt like that about, I mean."

"They haven't got any business—" the partner started to say.

"And you," Jim says, "you haven't got no heart. Not in poker," he says. "And not in police work."

"What I got is sense," the partner says.

"There's such a thing as too much sense," Jim says.

"Which you're not likely to have."

"Huh," Jim says. "I'm gonna whip you in that next game," he says. "If I got to wear a mask."

"Well, you got to, baby."

"Listen," Jim says to Arch and me. "How long will it take you to get over there? To the shop?"

"Ten minutes," I says. I couldn't hardly keep from grinnin'. I nudged Arch. He *did* grin.

"Right by the monkeys," Arch says. "That's where you might lose it. By those cages over by the door."

"You better believe I mean it," Jim says. "When I say to be careful. I'll skin your hides if you get into trouble."

"We'll take care," I says. "Don't you worry none."

NINE

It musta took us five hours to get over there to that
house. In Beverly Hills. We took our bike. Which is to
say, Arch's bike. But I use it anytime I want. So we call
it our bike.

First, Arch, he'd pedal a while. While I sat on the
crossbar. Then me, I'd pedal, while he sat on the crossbar. Then we'd walk a while. We'd take turns pushin'
the bike.

I bet we stopped at every gas station between our
place and Beverly Hills. Not to get no gas. No. Just to
drink up their free ice water.

It was dark night, when we got there. The street-
lights was on. Makin' long, dark shadows acrost the
lawns. Little puddles of yellow light under the lamp-
posts. And big black shadows everywhere else. The
houses was big and dark. With just a light in a window
here and there.

There wasn't nobody out. Where we live, you know?

They's people just everywhere. But out there in Beverly Hills, you don't see no people. Ain't that funny? You'd think they'd want to show off their nice clothes and big cars and that. But they ain't no one around. Not no one.

Anyway, this house, the one where Jimmy Hines, he said this guy lived. It was big, too. And dark. Made out of some kind of square-cut brown rock. Or like that. They was big trees all around it. Great big ellum trees, they looked like. Hangin' like long black hair over the roof. And black bushes all around the bottom of the house. It was scary enough.

It was a big ol' place. I mean big. It just went *on* bein' a house, back as far as you could see. But it was rundown, like. The grass growed up knee-high to a Chickashay. And they was this For Sale sign out in the middle of the tall grass.

You could hear the crickets, boy. They was singin' away like a sawmill in wintertime. And off up in a tree somewhere they was this locust, kind of leadin' the music. It sounded sad. And kinda lost. Up in the top story of the house, one window was broke. It looked like an eye with a patch over it.

Old Arch and me, we just stood acrost the street, lookin' at it. For a long time. You know, just lookin'. And not sayin' a word.

"You sure that it?" Arch said to me.

"Like it says on the paper. You saw it."

"There ain't no light."

"Around in back there is. Can't you see it? Just the one light? Over that there wall?"

"Oh, yeah, yeah."

"Well," I said.

"Well," Arch said.

"Come on," I said.

"We ain't gonna find out nothin' here."

"We got to *try*. For old Pest and Mrs. Zimmerman."

"Sure," Arch said. "Did I say we ain't gonna try? I didn't say that. You come on then."

We snuck acrost the street. Like two ghosts. Whush. Acrost the street and through that tall grass and in amongst them big ellum trees. You couldn't hear nothing. Not nothin' but our pants whisperin' through the grass. And a twig or two snappin', like.

First, we huddled up behind this tree.

"We got to get over that wall," Arch says.

"It's pretty high."

"Yeah. You remember that thing we did down at Ella Wheeler Wilcox? When we was doin' them army things?"

64

"You mean over the backstop?"

"Yeah. I get over there, under the wall. Then you run, right? And I grab your foot, right? And boost you up?"

"Yeah," I says. I kind of shivered.

"Well, okay."

So old Arch, he gets off under that big high wall. Musta been ten feet high or more. And I rared back, behind that tree, to make a run.

I come thunderin' acrost that grass, lickety-split. And I step into Arch's hands, all right. And he boosts me, all right. But somethin' went wrong. I don't know what. What I know is, I hit that wall with my face. And I bounced off. And I was lyin' on the ground. Flat on my back.

"Hey, man," Arch whispers. "You okay?"

"Oh, it's nothin'," I says. "Maybe a busted nose and two or three teeth gone. But nothin' real serious."

"Let's try it again."

"You think I'm crazy?"

"Pest," he says. Just that one word.

So I got up and went back. And rared back again. And made my run again. And this time my chest hit that wall flat. But my fingers grabbed the top. And old Arch, he give me a boost up. And I got to the top of the wall.

I rested like that for a minute. Hangin' by my finger-tips. Then I jumped up and grabbed the far side of the wall and let my arms lay acrost the top. And I dropped my legs down so's Arch could grab 'em. He grabbed 'em. And he started comin' up. Crawlin' up me like I was a rope or like that. And all this time my arms, they was diggin' into that concrete. Man. I tell you for fair. It *hurt*.

"Hey," Arch whispers, "there's a tree over there. That we can shinny down."

So we stood up and walked down that tall, narrow wall. It made me a little dizzy, there in the dark. And first Arch, then me, we swung out to a limb of that tree. Then we shinnied down that limb and down the trunk to the dark ground. Into the bushes.

"Whoa," Arch says, high and tight. "We got company."

"What?"

"Right in front of your face, man."

And sure enough. They was two of the biggest Doberman dogs you ever did see. They was just standin' there, lookin' interested.

"How come they ain't eating us up?" I whispered.

"They maybe smelled that dog all over our clothes," Arch, he says. "Or maybe it was that hex sign."

"What hex sign?"

"The one my Aunt May, she gave me."

"Let me see it."

"Some other time, man, you don't mind?" Arch, he stuck out a hand. And the front dog, he licked the hand. Just nice. "There, boy," Arch says. "You just go on bein' good. Huh?"

We made good friends with them dogs. Then we moved off down the yard. Toward this big lighted window. They was curtains acrost it. But right in the middle, the curtains, they was drawed back a little.

Now, to get up and look in that window you had to climb this iron rail. It was maybe six feet up and two, three feet out from the big window. Off to the side, they was these two little windows. The kind that swings open? You know? And one of them, it was open just a hair.

So to *see,* one of us, he had to climb up the rail in the middle. And to *hear,* the other one, he had to climb up the rail on the end.

Arch went up on the middle of the rail, first. He had to kind of balance there, between these two posts with sharp ends.

"You see anybody?"

"It's him," Arch whispers. "I see that guy."

"What's he doin'?"

"He's talkin' to this white girl."

"Yeah?"

"I can't hear 'em. And they's another guy. A young guy. *Two* other guys. Not much older'n you and me."

"Yeah?"

"Get down there and listen," he whispers.

So I went down to the end and climbed up. Me, I could balance better. I could reach over and put my hand against the wall. Old Arch, he couldn't quite reach the glass.

I could hear these voices. This girl, she says, "So what you gonna do, Joe?"

"We'll take the truck out," this deep voice says. "And cart 'em over to Arizona tomorrow night. All of them doped, of course."

"And I meet you up there?" the girl says. "At Arrowhead?"

"Yeah. You bring the car."

That was all I heard, before I heard Arch kind of gasp. I looked over at him. He was kinda half fallin' back. You know? Windmilling his arms around, like. He wobbled back. Then he wobbled to the front. He did that twice. Then he kind of dived through that there plate glass window.

Them Doberman dogs, they set to barkin'. Lord God, I thought the sky, it was a-fallin'. I tell you, my heart scrunched up. And I couldn't hardly breathe.

"Hey man," I yells, "you all right?" No use whisperin' anymore, was they? No. "You all right?"

"Yeah, yeah," he hollers. "I'm all right. You get outa here."

But I teetered down that rail, first. To look in and make sure. There was Arch, sittin' in the middle of the floor. And there was the mean guy. And the two young guys. And the girl. All standin' up lookin' at him. Surprised, like.

But they wasn't too surprised. One of the young ones, he had out this automatic pistol. Yeah. Pointin' it at Arch. And the big guy, he says, "Get out there and get that other one. Quick."

Now them Dobermans. That breakin' glass and all the noise, it got them excited. I jumped off that rail and they was after me. You never seen a boy run half that fast. I was acrost that grass and up into that tree, *fast*. I mean. All I lost was one pants leg. And a little hide off my left calf. I was up that tree and over that wall and down. Faster'n you could say it.

And acrost the street to where our bike was hid in this big bush. I got into that bush myself. Under the branches.

I just laid there, gettin' my breath. I was gonna leave. But then I couldn't. Because first, this young guy comes out of that house acrost the street. With this gun, still in his hand. Then the other young guy, holdin' Arch. Then the girl and the big guy.

They all got into this station wagon that was parked in the driveway. All of 'em.

And I had to lay there and watch them wheel away with my best friend. Old Arch. He looked kinda shook up and scared. They passed right under a streetlight. And I could see his face. He was bleedin' from two or three cuts. And he looked kinda scared.

I tell you, I never felt worse in my life. First it was Pest gone. Now it was Arch. And I didn't even have the chance to tell old Arch good-bye.

TEN

"I told you," Jim Hines said. "I told you to stay out of trouble."

"We tried," I said. "But old Arch, he fell through that window."

"And they took him?" I was on the telephone, talkin' to Jim.

It was three in the mornin', about. I don't know. I just know it took me almost as long to go back. I mean from Beverly Hills to over by my house. At the corner gas station. Because us, we haven't got a phone in our house. And just as long almost to get old Jim's home phone number. They didn't want to give it to me down at the Glass House. Which is what they call the downtown police station.

"Why didn't you tell the Beverly Hills police?" Jim, he said.

"Are they any good?"

Jim laughed. "They all right. Of course, they ain't

the L.A. Department. But they'll do. Anyway, this is kidnappin', now. It ain't just dogs anymore."

"Yeah," I said. "You mean they'll do somethin'?"

"Why, course they will. What you think? We gonna let that boy just get took off?"

"I didn't think nothin'. I just knew I had to call you."

"Well, you wait there. I'll pick you up."

So I sat there. In this all-night fillin' station. Wonderin' if Arch, he was still alive. Cryin' a little. I admit it. I cried some. I sat there and stared at the gas pumps and the oil cans. And I felt bad.

ELEVEN

"I told you I can't work up at Arrowhead. That's for the county boys. The Sheriff's Department. I told you and told you." Jim and me was in his car. In this dark station.

"You maybe can't go," I tell him. "But me, I can."

"How you gonna get there?"

"I'll hitch. I'll walk. I'll crawl. But I'm goin'."

Jim heaves this big sigh. "Well," he says. "You go off up there by yourself, you'll get in trouble again. I know that."

"I won't."

"Nothin' says a private citizen can't go to Arrowhead," Jim says. "Even a cop."

"You mean it?"

"I can take you up there," Jim says. "And we can look around. But that's all. You hear me?"

TWELVE

"Are you sure it's broke?" I says.

Jimmy Hines kind of gasped. "Yeah," he says. "I'm sure. I broke an arm once, I was a kid."

It was old Jim's leg, this time. We was lyin' up on this big rock, up among some pines. That's where Jim fell. We was comin' down this hill, between the trees, and he slipped on some pine needles. He just flipped, and he went downhill too fast to stop.

And just when we found the place. There it was, down there in a little canyon. Down under the rock. Where we could see them. But they couldn't see us. There was this cabin. And behind it, this big pen with a bunch of dogs. And Pest was there. I could see him.

Pest, he looked bad. There wasn't no food dishes in this little bitty pen. And there wasn't no water. Nor nothing else. Except this big pack of dogs, kind of jammed together. Pest, he was layin' down. Lookin' sick and kind of weak.

How we got there? We asked around at Arrowhead. How about this red Buick? And the guy that owned it? And the two young guys and the girl? It took us hours before a guy at a gas station told us something. *He* just knew they went up one road.

Jim and me, we took this road all the way. It kinda petered out in the pines and underbrush. Or it looked that way. What it was, there was this trail that the road turned into, kind of. And they was fresh-cut brush covering it up. So we just followed it.

We almost run smack into the cabin. But a dog barked. And so Jim and me, we went up the hill. To look around. That was when Jim slipped and broke his left ankle. Both bones, it looked like. Or that's what Jim said. Turned out later he was right, too.

"You cain't walk at all?"

"No," Jim says. "And I'm too heavy to lean on you. What we got to do, you got to go back to Arrowhead. Can you drive?"

"Sure. A little." Truth was, I never had drove. But I couldn't tell that to Jim.

"Okay. Go back to where we hid the car. See?"

"Yeah."

"And you scoot back down to Arrowhead. And you call the sheriff's station. Here." Jim took some change and a five out of his pocket. "Take this. In case you need some money."

"Okay," I says.

"Wait." Jim points. "Look there."

Down there, the cabin door, it opened. And out comes one of them young guys. Holdin' a big rifle. He stood out there and looked around for a minute. Kind of sniffin'. Three or four dogs started barkin'. And old Pest, he raised his head and looked around.

"He's goin' back in," Jim says. "You get to cuttin'."

"Yeah," I says.

That was when this window broke. Down in the cabin. There was this one big window. On our side. It busted, loud and sudden. With a crash and a clatter. And out come who?

Old Arch, that's who. He come sailin' out that window and landed on the dirt. On his shoulder and knee. Because his hands was tied.

He was up and runnin', quick. He cut out up the hill, ziggin' and zaggin'.

But this guy, see. The one with the rifle? He was at the busted window. And aimin' down on old Arch.

I couldn't help it, man. I stood up and I yells. "Hey, Arch," I yells, "get behind that there rock!"

But it didn't do no good. All it done, it slowed old

Arch down. I hate to think about it, to this minute. That I slowed old Arch down.

Because this rifle, it whinged. And Arch, he flips over. And, Lord God, I thought he was dead. He rolled over behind this rock and he just laid there. My heart, it squoze up like an old sour sponge.

I was still standin' there. Like a fool. "Arch," I yells, "say somethin'."

"Hello," Archie yells. Then he gives this here little strangled laugh.

Which kind of made me mad. "You crazy idiot," I yells, "I thought you was dead."

"I ain't even sick," Arch yells back. "I'm all right."

"We gonna come down and get you, man!"

"Naw," Arch yells.

Jim pulls at my arm. "Get down," he hisses. And just then, whing, whang!! Two shots, they whistle by. And me, I ducked. You better believe it.

And huh-row! The world blows up right by my left ear. I shook my head and turned and looked at Jim. Who I thought for sure had been blowed up.

But what it was, he had out this .38. And he was cuttin' away at this young guy. Who come out the door and headed for Arch.

"I didn't know you had no gun," I says.

"Lot of things you don't know. Now, shut up. I got to concentrate. I ain't exactly the world's best shot." Jim squinches up his eyes. And levels down on this guy down there.

"You got another gun?"

Jim turned and looked at me. "How I gonna shoot if you keep yappin'? Huh? You stop to think about that? No. I haven't got another gun. I *did,* you wouldn't get it."

"I can shoot."

Down there, while we was talkin', this young guy was about over to where Arch was. Out in this dirt clearing. You know? Kinda crouched over, like that would help any.

Huh-row! Huh-row! That .38 bucked in Jim's hands. And dirt, it exploded around the guy's feet, down there. He got the funniest look on his face. And he stopped. He stopped and looked back at the cabin. And up to us. And back to the cabin. Then he dropped his rifle. And with this silly sausage-eatin' grin, he lifts up his hands.

Jim laughs. "Stay where you're at," he yells.

"You stay where you're at," this rough voice behind us says. Which turned me cold, I mean. Like a whole tribe of Eskimos was walkin' up my back, barefoot.

Jim he got this hurt look on his face. "How dumb can a guy get?" he mutters to himself.

"Throw it over your shoulder," the guy says. It was Joe, the big guy. Standin' there with another rifle in his hands. I knew 'cause I turned around and looked.

Jim just sighed and flang his pistol over his shoulder. It plopped down in the pine needles.

"Now get up and walk," Joe says. Oh, he looked mean.

"I can't walk," Jim says.

"You got to."

"I can't, man!"

"Then crawl."

And Joe, he made him do it. He made old Jim drag himself off of that rock and down that slope. It took us twenty minutes. Jim, he was sweatin' and gruntin'. But he didn't holler. He didn't so much as groan.

They was all out when we got down there. Joe. And the two young guys. And the girl. And they had Arch, too. Out in the dirt, in front the cabin.

There was Jim, stretched out on the ground. And Joe, lookin' mean, with this rifle. And one of the other guys, with Jim's .38. And the girl, kind of grinnin'.

"Wow," she says. "Sounded like the Battle of Gettysburg. What'll you do with all of them?"

"What would you do?" Joe says.

"Tie them up and leave them."

"And let them send the cops after us?"

"You think they won't come anyway?" The girl, she laughs. She was a cool one.

Me, I wasn't so cool. I wasn't shakin'. But just about. I was scared. I mean.

"You, kid," Joe says to me. "How come you came up here?"

"To get my buddy," I says, nodding at Arch, who grinned at me.

"How'd you know where to come?"

"I heard you say Arrowhead. Through the window."

"Yeah," Joe says. "Now, how'd you find the house? In Beverly Hills."

I didn't say nothin'. He walked over and slapped me. Not hard. But hard enough.

"How'd you find us?"

I didn't say nothin'.

Joe, he raised his hand to hit me again. But Jim spoke up. "I told him. I'm a police officer."

"Fuzz?" Joe says. "Well, that kills it. Are there more out there?"

"Two more cars coming," Jim says. Which was a lie. They wasn't no more cars. Not anywhere.

"Yeah?" Joe says. "How come you aren't in uniform?"

"I'm a detective."

"Let me see your I.D."

Jim dragged his billfold out, slow. And he handed it over. Joe looked at it. "You ain't even a sergeant," he says. "You're just a plain cop. Isn't that right?"

Jim didn't say a word.

"And why would you bring this kid along? If you were on duty. Nah. You just came up. Why?"

Nobody said a thing.

"Oh, it doesn't matter," Joe says. He looked thoughtful. "We got to kill them," he says, then.

"What?" the girl says. "Are you crazy?"

Joe shakes his head. "That's the only way." He turns to the guy, the other young one. "Take them up in the gulley," he says. "Where the trash hole is. And shoot 'em."

The other young guy looks at him. "Not me," he says. "No."

"Joe," the girl says. She laid her pretty white hand on his arm. "Listen," she says. "You kill these guys, and you have got a big problem on your hands. You know how cops are. When you kill another cop."

Joe, he thinks about that.

86

"If you tie them up," the girl says, "and leave them. Just leave them up there."

"And gag 'em good." Joe nods.

"Might as well kill us," Jim says. "Exposure, that would kill us anyway. Inside of two or three days."

"But that way," the girl says, "we didn't do it." She winked at me. "See, Joe?"

"Yeah," Joe says. "Why I got talked into this stupid business is beyond me," he says. *"Now* look."

"You might as well shoot us now," Jim says.

The girl gave him a mean, dirty look. And I kicked his ankle. Turned out, it was the bad one. Jim, he moaned and looked like he wanted to finish me off himself. But he shut his big mouth.

So Joe, he had two young guys get rope to tie us all up. And some old sheet that I knowed was gonna taste just awful for a gag. Then them two young guys, they started haulin' Jim up around the cabin. And Arch and me, we followed, with Joe behind us. Around the cabin and up the hill we went. To die.

THIRTEEN

It all happened fast. I can tell you that.

We was goin' around the cabin, see? Around past the dog pen. Now, this pen. It had a chicken wire fence, maybe six feet high. And all the dogs was in it.

We come around the corner of the cabin. And there was old Pest. He was standin' up now. Not lookin' too good. But up and kinda braced. Like he knowed we was in trouble.

'Bout that time, old Arch, he stumbled. And this Joe, he takes a cut at Arch with his rifle. Cracks him on the shoulder. And Arch lets out a yell. He wasn't expectin' it, see.

Old Pest, I swear. He seen that. And he growled, deep in his throat. And he whirled and run to the backside of that pen. Then he run for that fence.

I don't think Joe even seen him. I mean, he wasn't watchin' that fence. He wasn't thinkin' about dogs. He had too much else to think about. Fact is, I think he was

sick of dogs at that point.

But old Pest was watchin' Joe. He come at that fence a mile a minute. And he sailed up. He didn't clear it. No. He hit the top with his belly. But his front feet were across. And he scrambled on over. He fell on his side, in the dirt. But he was up, fast.

He was up and runnin' at Joe. Who saw him now. Who raised up his rifle and cut down on Pest. Joe, I mean. But not fast enough. Pest was all over him. He slashed at his rifle arm. The rifle dropped.

Then he was up at Joe's throat. And Joe was down on the ground, yellin'.

"Shoot him," he yells at this guy with Jim's .38. But that guy just stood there with his mouth open. He was, anyway, holdin' up Jim. Who grabbed him. By the throat and flung him over. Jim, I mean, he grabbed the young guy.

And the .38 shot out of the young guy's hand and flipped through the air.

Guess who was after it?

Me, that's who. And I got it pretty fast, too. I grabbed it up and cocked it and whirled around.

"Pest!" I yells. "Hey, Pest! Come!" Because he woulda killed Joe. I mean. He took a couple more bites. Then he let go and come over to me. His tail waggin' and a big grin on. Oh, it was good to see him again. I hugged him, big. And he licked my face.

And Arch, he had the rifle. Joe's rifle, I mean. And all of a sudden, it was all over. Because the young guy, he give up quick. It was that or get choked by old Jimmy Hines. And the girl and the other guy, they had run off. We could hear a car startin' around the corner.

"They'll get them two," Jim says. "Let's tie these guys up and get a doctor up here."

I looked over at Arch. "You all right, man?" I says.

"I'll live."

And he did, too.

FOURTEEN

It was the next day we went over to Mrs. Zimmerman's. The pet shop, I mean.

They was this man there. In a nice suit and tie. A kind of rough lookin' guy. But with nice eyes.

"Boys," Mrs. Zimmerman said. "I got news for you."

"What's that?" Arch said.

Old Pest, he was actin' kind of funny. Whinin' and sniffin' and pullin' over to this fellow. On his leash.

"Hello, Ritter," the guy said. And he patted old Pest on the head. And stroked him down the shoulder.

"His name is Pest," I said.

"That's what I got to tell you, boys," Mrs. Zimmerman said. "This is Mr. Horner."

And we all shook hands real polite. Except I wasn't feelin' polite. My stomach, it was flutterin'. And I had this kinda sick feelin', all over.

"It's some bad news," Mrs. Zimmerman said. "And some good."

"I guess Mr. Horner, he really owns Pest," I said. Or kinda whispered.

"Yes," Mrs. Zimmerman said. And Mr. Horner, he smiled at me.

"He is the dog's legal owner," Mrs. Zimmerman said. "And I know you think that's bad. Right?"

"Right." I smiled kind of apologetic at the guy. Mr. Horner.

"But Mr. Horner owns big, big kennels. And lots of other things. But the kennels."

"Yeah?" Arch stuck his hands in his pants pockets.

"Mr. Horner needs a manager. And he asked me would I do it. Of course I would," Mrs. Zimmerman said.

I looked at Arch, sad. Then at Mrs. Zimmerman. And I tried to smile. Because, honest, I was happy for her. But what about Pest? You mean I almost got killed to save him? Just to get him took away? I asked myself that.

"Now about Ritter, or Pest, or whatever his name is."

"I just have to have him, boys," Mr. Horner said. He sounded sorry to say it. "He's champion breeding stock. Four of his sons and daughters are champions."

Arch and me looked at each other. We didn't know Pest was a daddy.

"But I was wondering," Mr. Horner said, "if you boys couldn't help out at the kennels. The pay would be good. And Pest would be just like your dog. Except that he'd stay around."

I looked at Arch. And Arch, he looked at me. "Sure," I said. And Arch said the same. "I guess," I said. "If my old man, he says it's all right."

"And boys," Mr. Horner said. "I wouldn't have my dog back except that you saved him. The next litter at the kennel, you can have your pick. Any pup you want."

So that's how it all happened. All about Pest.

Most other people now, they call him Ritter von Bulow the Third. Which is his legal name, all right. But Arch and me, we call him Pest. And he's our dog.

So is Ritter von Bulow the Fourth. Who is our dog, even legal and all like that. Even if we do just call him Nip. Because that's what he mostly does.

So you can see it worked out all right. Old Jimmy Hines, his leg healed up all right. And he's back on the force. And Joe, he's up for kidnapping Arch and Jim and me. And the other two guys, too. They never did catch that girl. Jim says they will. But they haven't yet.

But Arch and me, we don't care. We got Pest and we got Nip. And we got a good job. We practice our hittin' and pitchin' and fieldin' almost every day. And we're

savin' our money. To go to college and learn to be vets. You know. Animal doctors. If the Dodgers don't give us a contract or like that.